PRINCESS

Don't miss any of these other stories by Ellen Miles!

THE PUPPY PLACE
Goldie
Snowball
Shadow
Rascal
Buddy
Flash
Scout
Patches
Noodle
Pugsley
Princess
Maggie and Max

TAYLOR-MADE TALES
The Dog's Secret
The Pirate's Plot
The Cowgirl's Luck
The Penguin's Peril

SCHOLASTIC JUNIOR CLASSICS
Doctor Dolittle
The Pied Piper
The Twelve Dancing Princesses
The Wind in the Willows

THE PUPPY PLACE

PRINCESS

ELLEN MILES

SCHOLASTIC INC.

New York   Toronto   London   Auckland   Sydney
Mexico City   New Delhi   Hong Kong   Buenos Aires

No part of this publication may be reproduced, stored in a retrieval system, or transmitted in any form or by any means, electronic, mechanical, photocopying, recording, or otherwise, without written permission of the publisher. For information regarding permission, write to Scholastic Inc., Attention: Permissions Department, 557 Broadway, New York, NY 10012.

ISBN-13: 978-0-545-03458-6
ISBN-10: 0-545-03458-2

Cover art by Tim O'Brien
Design by Steve Scott

12 11 10 9 8 7 6 5 4 3 2   8 9 10 11 12 13/0

Printed in the U.S.A.

First printing, March 2008

CHAPTER ONE

"Okay, Charles. Your turn!" Danielle pointed to the big chair. "Have a seat, sir. What's it going to be today? A Mohawk, maybe? Buzz cut?" Charles climbed into the chair and settled in. Danielle shook out a big black nylon cape and fastened it at the back of his neck so it covered his shoulders and chest.

Charles laughed. "Just the usual, I guess." He smiled into the mirror at his own reflection and Danielle's.

Danielle had been the Peterson family's regular haircutter for as long as Charles could remember. Her shop used to be right in downtown Littleton, next to the library, but last year she had moved to this place — called Hair Today —

1

which was three towns over. So Mom made all their appointments on the same day: for herself, for Charles, for his older sister, Lizzie, and for his little brother, Adam (who everybody *always* called the Bean). They would all drive over together and then head back home together an hour or so later, enjoying what Mom called "that spiffy brand-new haircut feeling."

Dad got his hair cut by Bernie, down at the fire station where he worked. "It's convenient," Dad said, "and the price is right." Meaning, it was free. But Bernie's haircuts were sometimes a little weird, and often Mom had to use her sewing scissors to "even things up" afterward, so Dad wouldn't go around looking like he'd just rolled out of bed.

Charles liked Danielle because she loved to laugh and because she always wore wild outfits, like purple high-top sneakers with pink polka-dotted tights. He liked it when she washed his hair with lots of warm water and her special lemony shampoo that smelled so good he almost wanted to eat it. He even liked waiting around in the salon while everybody else got their hair cut.

Charles sometimes felt funny about being the only boy in the place. (The Bean didn't really count, since he was so little.) But so what if he was? It just meant that he got lots of smiles and attention from all the ladies sitting under hair dryers or getting their nails done.

Still, maybe it wouldn't be so great if one of the guys from school walked by and saw him in there, happily reading a magazine and eating the dainty sugar cookies Danielle always offered. Maybe Charles would be totally embarrassed if word got around that he hung out at a place like that. Maybe it was a good thing that Hair Today was all the way over in Springfield.

Now Danielle snipped away at the hair around Charles's ears. *Snick-snick!* She was so quick. But she had never cut him with her sharp scissors, not even once, not even a tiny nick. "So, how's that adorable Buddy? Has he had any foster

3

brothers or sisters lately?" she asked. She loved hearing about the Petersons' puppy and about the other puppies that the family took care of.

The Petersons had been fostering puppies for a while before Buddy came along. Until Buddy, Charles's mom and dad had said that the family was not ready for a dog of their own. But Charles and Lizzie and the Bean *loved* dogs, so their parents had agreed to let them take care of puppies who needed temporary homes. That's what "fostering" meant.

Each puppy only stayed a little while, just until the Petersons could find it the perfect forever family. But when Buddy came along, everybody knew right away that they could never, never let him go. The *Petersons* were Buddy's perfect forever family.

Buddy was brown, with big brown eyes and a heart-shaped white spot on his chest. He was cute, smart, and a ton of fun to play with. Charles had always imagined that having a puppy of his own would be the best thing that ever happened to him. And with Buddy, that had turned out to be true.

But it was still fun to foster other puppies. Now Charles told Danielle all about Noodle, the most recent puppy his family had fostered. Noodle was a poodle–golden retriever mix that the Petersons had helped to rescue after Lizzie spotted him swimming, way out in the middle of icy Loon Lake!

"Noodle sounds like a great puppy," Danielle said. "I bet your sister was crazy about him. Lizzie loves those big dogs, doesn't she?"

It was true. Charles knew that it had not been easy for Lizzie to give Noodle up when the time came.

"But now that your family has Buddy, it's a little easier to see the other puppies come and go, right?" Danielle snipped a tiny bit above Charles's forehead.

"Definitely." Charles was going to nod, but he remembered just in time that he was supposed to keep his head still while Danielle was working.

Danielle stood back to take a look at her work. "I think you're all done!" she said. She held up a mirror so Charles could see the back of his own head, reflected in the bigger mirror on the wall. "What do you think?" she asked. "Like it?"

"Sure!" said Charles. His hair didn't really look any different: just a little shorter and a little neater. Perfect. "Thanks, Danielle."

Danielle spun Charles around in the chair, then unsnapped the cape and swept it away. Tiny bits of Charles's hair flew off to join the other clippings on the floor. "Ta-da!" she said. "Now, where's that Bean?" She scanned the room.

Near the front door, a little knot of women — some with weird tinfoil thingies in their hair, others wearing curlers or plastic-wrap turbans — surrounded someone who had just come in. Charles had not heard the bells jingle, but now he saw that Angela, one of Hair Today's other stylists, had just arrived. The Bean, who was always curious, had run over to join the crowd. He stood near the edge, trying to push his way in. "Me 'scuze! Me 'scuze!" he kept saying.

But the women were too busy oohing and aah-ing over something to hear him. Charles saw them reaching out toward Angela as if they were trying to touch whatever it was she was holding.

"What's going on?" Charles asked Danielle. "Did she bring in a baby or something?"

Danielle rolled her eyes and shook her head. "Not exactly."

Just then, one of the women stepped aside so Charles could see what Angela was holding in her arms. It was a puppy! A very, *very* small puppy, with silky brown-and-black hair that was touched with silver. It had the tiniest black nose and eyes, and a big pink bow right on top of its head. The puppy was wearing a tiny white T-shirt that said MOMMY'S LITTLE GIRL, in shiny pink script.

"That," Danielle told Charles, "would be Princess. Otherwise known as the most spoiled dog in the history of the universe."

CHAPTER TWO

Charles barely heard what Danielle said about Princess. As soon as he saw the puppy, he was on his feet and on his way over to get a closer look. He had never *seen* such a tiny dog! She was unbelievably cute, like a little stuffed toy.

The puppy looked back at him with sparkly black eyes. Her little ears perked up.

Great, another fan! Hello there! Want to pat me?

Lizzie joined Charles near the crowd of women. "Huh. A Yorkie," she said. "Cute, I guess. If you like little dogs. I don't know why people have to dress them up in T-shirts, though."

"What kind of dog did you say it is?" Charles asked his sister. His eyes were glued to the puppy in Angela's arms.

"Yorkshire terrier. It'll get bigger than that, but not much." Lizzie didn't sound impressed. She was not a big fan of any dog smaller than, say, Patches, a beagle puppy the Petersons had recently fostered.

Mom had come over to help the Bean work his way to the front of the crowd so he could see the puppy. "Okay, pal," she said to the Bean now. "Your turn for a haircut. Danielle's all ready for you."

"But the uppy —" The Bean reached out his arms toward the puppy.

"Not now," Mom said firmly. She pulled the Bean away and walked him over to Danielle's chair.

Charles was so busy looking at the puppy that he had hardly noticed what Angela was saying. Now he realized that she was upset about something — or was she happy? She was sort of laughing and crying at the same time.

"I just heard the good news this morning!" Charles heard her say. "I've been accepted to study with on*ree*!"

Charles had no idea what on*ree* was. But all the women gasped. "On*ree*!" they echoed. "Ooh!"

Charles edged closer to Lizzie. "What's on*ree*?" he asked.

Lizzie snorted. "First of all, it's *who*, not *what*," she said. "Second of all, it's a *name*, spelled H-E-N-R-I. Pronounced 'On*ree*,' with the accent on the second syllable. It's French for Henry."

"Okay, fine." Charles rolled his eyes. Lizzie could be *such* a know-it-all. "So, *who's* Henri?"

Lizzie waved to get Angela's attention. "Um, who's Henri?"

Ha! So Lizzie didn't know *everything*. But she was never shy when it came to asking questions. Charles was curious, too, but he would never have spoken right up like that.

"Henri? He's just the most famous, most creative, most amazing colorist in the universe, that's all!" Angela's cheeks were pink and her eyes were bright with excitement.

"Colorist? Like — with crayons?" Charles pictured the Bean hard at work at the kitchen table, creating one of his scrawly, loopy drawings. Was the Bean a colorist?

Angela laughed. "No, like for hair," she said. "There's nobody better than Henri when it comes to dyeing hair. All the movie stars adore him. They won't go to anyone else." She took a deep breath. "And now I, Angela McKnight, am going to Los Angeles, California, to study with him! I leave *tomorrow*. It's the most amazing, the most wonderful, the most *incredible* thing that's ever happened!"

She put her face down to nuzzle her puppy, and when she looked up again, there were tears in her eyes. "And the worst thing that's ever happened, too." She wiped her eyes and gave a huge sniff. "I'm going to have to give up my darling baby girl, my Princess."

"Why?" one of the women asked. "Can't you take her with you?"

Angela shook her head. "I'll be studying with Henri all day long, every day. Who would look after her? Princess needs a lot of attention." She nuzzled the top of the puppy's head again. "Don't you, sweetie? Momma's wittle cupcake needs wots and wots of wove."

Princess licked Angela's nose.

Whatever. Just keep the love coming!

Charles and Lizzie exchanged a glance, and Lizzie pretended to gag. They both *hated* it when people spoke baby talk to their dogs.

"How long will you be gone?" another woman asked. "Maybe you could find someone to take care of Princess for a while."

Angela shook her head. "The truth is, I don't think I'll be coming back. I've always wanted to live in California, and this is my big chance!"

12

The women started asking more questions about Henri, but Charles slipped away to find Mom. She was over at Danielle's station, supervising the Bean's haircut. "Maybe a little more off the back," Mom was saying as Danielle snipped away at the Bean's soft curls.

"Mom?" Charles asked. "Can we —"

"Don't tell me you're asking if we can foster that little brat," Lizzie said, coming up behind him.

Charles couldn't believe it. "That's not nice!" he told his sister. "Just because you don't like little dogs doesn't mean we shouldn't help this one out, just like we'd help any puppy who needed us." Spoiled or not, Charles thought Princess was really, really cute. He was *dying* to have her stay with his family until they could find her a new home.

"It's not that I dislike *all* little dogs," Lizzie said. "Snowball was okay. So was Rascal. But *this* one! She's tiny *and* spoiled. I can tell already by the way Angela cuddles her and baby talks

13

to her. Not to mention that T-shirt she's got her wearing!"

Mom was shaking her head. "I don't know, Charles. Lizzie might be right about this puppy. Princess might need more attention than we have time to give." She looked at Charles, and he looked back at her with big, sad eyes, imitating the "poor little puppy" look that sometimes worked for Buddy when he was hoping for a pat or a treat.

It seemed to work for Charles, too.

Mom sighed. "But you're right, too. If we call ourselves a foster family, that means we should help out any puppy that needs us." She pulled out her cell phone and called Dad.

Charles crossed his fingers while he listened to Mom's side of the conversation. "It's a Yorkie," she was saying. "Yes, one of those little yappy — I know, I know, but Charles likes her, and we should help if we can, and —"

She hung up and sighed again. "Well, he agreed. I can't believe *I'm* talking *Dad* into taking in a puppy." Then she winked at Charles. Mom was really more of a cat person, but Charles could tell that she thought Princess was cute. Yay! Charles could hardly wait.

By the time they left Hair Today, Angela had agreed to let the Petersons foster Princess. In fact, she was going to bring the puppy over that very night. "We'll need some time, so I can tell you all about how to take care of her," she said. "And of course, I'll bring the List."

CHAPTER THREE

"Uh-oh. She mentioned a list?" Aunt Amanda shook her head. "That could mean trouble." It was later that same day, back at the Petersons'. Princess had not arrived yet, but Charles's aunt Amanda had stopped by to say hello on her way home from a long day at work, and Charles was telling her all about the Yorkie that was coming to visit.

Aunt Amanda was Dad's little sister. Charles always tried to imagine Dad and Aunt Amanda when they were his and Lizzie's age. Dad had once told him that Aunt Amanda reminded him a lot of Lizzie. So maybe when Aunt Amanda was Lizzie's age she was bossy, too.

But even if she *was* bossy then, now she was

nice. Charles liked her a lot, and he loved to visit her at Bowser's Backyard, her doggy day care center, where she took care of dogs whose owners worked all day and didn't have time to play with them. Lizzie worked there one day a week, and she said she learned a lot every time. Charles thought Aunt Amanda might be the only person in the universe who knew more about dogs than Lizzie did.

Now Aunt Amanda and Charles were sitting on the Petersons' back deck, watching her dogs tear around the backyard with Buddy. Aunt Amanda and Uncle James had *four* dogs altogether: three pugs and one golden retriever. The Petersons had fostered Pugsley, one of the pugs. Pugsley, also known as Mr. Pest, had been a real handful. And he still was! But Aunt Amanda and Uncle James were the perfect forever family for him, because they loved him anyway. And he got along great with all their other dogs.

Which was obvious right now. Pugsley was chasing Lionel and Jack, his two pug "brothers," while Bowser, the golden retriever, lay on his back letting Buddy pretend to beat him up. Then Pugsley ran over to jump on Bowser, too, and Lionel and Jack dashed after him. Soon Bowser was almost completely covered in pugs. He rolled over and jumped to his feet, giving himself a good shake. The smaller dogs tumbled down, somersaulted, and dashed off for their next adventure: barking at the cat next door.

Charles and Aunt Amanda laughed as they watched. "There's just something about pugs," Aunt Amanda said. "They keep you laughing, that's for sure."

Mom came outside carrying a tray loaded with crackers and cheese. Lizzie followed her, carrying a pitcher of Mom's famous lemonade. Behind Lizzie came the Bean, carrying a squeaky toy shaped like a hamburger. The Bean liked to pretend that he was a puppy, so most of his favorite toys were actually dog toys.

"Have a snack," Mom said to Aunt Amanda.

She poured a glass of lemonade and passed it over. "Now, what did I hear you say about Angela's List meaning 'trouble'?"

"Thanks!" Aunt Amanda took a sip of her lemonade before she answered the question. "*Mmm*, you make the best lemonade! Well, it's just that sometimes new customers bring a list when they drop off their dogs at day care. The list is always full of complicated instructions about how to take care of their dog. Some people can be very fussy about their dogs' likes and dislikes. And it's not just little dogs like this Princess that can be spoiled. That's a myth. People definitely spoil big dogs, too."

"For example?" Mom asked.

"For example, I have one customer at Bowser's Backyard who gives only bottled water to her golden retriever." Aunt Amanda raised an eyebrow as she took another sip of lemonade.

"Bottled water? For a dog?" Mom stared at her. "You're *kidding*."

"I'm not," said Aunt Amanda. "What's more, I follow her directions."

"Some dogs have very sensitive stomachs," Lizzie said. "If they drink different water from what they're used to, they can get an upset tummy."

"Absolutely correct," said Aunt Amanda. "And since I'm usually caring for thirty dogs at once, I don't have time to be cleaning up after one dog with an upset tummy, if you know what I mean." She smiled. "But the thing about these people with lists is, usually the people have *made* the dog into a fussy, picky creature. If you only give your dog bottled water, that's what your dog is going to get used to, and what it's going to expect. It's not the *dogs'* fault that they're spoiled. It's the people's fault."

Mom nodded. "Well, Angela should be here any minute to drop off Princess. We'll just have to wait and see what's on *her* list. Hopefully it won't be too complicated."

"Hopefully," echoed Aunt Amanda, smiling into her glass of lemonade. "Anyway, I almost forgot what I came over for. I wanted to see if either of you" — she looked at Charles and Lizzie — "would like to help me out with a new activity I'm going to be doing with Bowser. It's a program at the library called Reading With Rover."

"I've heard of that!" Lizzie said. "It's where kids read to dogs, right?"

"Exactly." Aunt Amanda nodded. "The program pairs kids who don't like reading, or who are having a hard time learning to read, with a dog and its owner. It seems that reading to a dog makes reading so much fun that the kids learn faster and end up doing better in school."

"That sounds wonderful," said Mom.

Aunt Amanda went on. "Bowser and I have just finished a training program, where we learned how to get kids motivated to read, and how to keep the dogs' attention on the kids. Bowser did pretty well when we practiced that part. He got rewarded with treats when he lay still to listen to me reading. Anyway, we'll go on Saturdays, and tomorrow we have our first session with a reader. I'm excited! But I think I could use some help making sure that Bowser stays calm and focused at the library."

Charles was just about to say he would help. He loved dogs, and he loved to read. The program sounded like a lot of fun.

But before he could say a thing, Lizzie spoke up. "I'll do it!" she said, waving her hand as if she were at school, hoping to be called on. Then, suddenly, she frowned. "Oops. Did you say tomorrow?" She put her hand back down and frowned. "I can't! Saturday's the day I volunteer at Caring Paws. Phooey!"

Lizzie worked one day a week at the local animal shelter, helping to take care of all the dogs and cats that were waiting to be adopted.

"Awww, too bad," Charles said cheerfully.

"Guess I'll do it instead!" Lizzie stuck out her tongue at him, but he didn't care. He was going to get to help Aunt Amanda!

Just then, the doorbell rang. "That must be Angela!" said Mom. They all got up and went to greet their new foster puppy.

When Mom opened the door, Angela was standing there clutching a pink plastic dog carrier in the shape of a palace, complete with three pink flags flying from three tall towers. Charles thought Angela looked as if she might have been crying, but now she put on a big smile. "Her Majesty has arrived!" said Angela, holding up the carrier so they could see inside. "Here's my wittle Pwincess!"

Princess sat inside the carrier, nestled on a silky pink blanket. She was wearing another T-shirt, this one with I'M A PRINCESS spelled out in pink glitter. There was a matching pink bow in her hair and — Charles could hardly believe his eyes — the puppy's teeny-tiny toenails were painted pink, too!

"And here," Angela said as she handed a thick stack of stapled-together papers to Mom, "is the List."

CHAPTER FOUR

FEEDING: Part One
A) Princess eats one food and one food only:
Marvelous Morsels.
The Beef-Bacon Bonanza flavor in the pink
can is the only one she likes.
B) Don't even try to give her the Creamy
Chicken Carnival (yellow can) or the Luscious
Lamb (green can) flavors. She will not
eat them.

"Well, that's just ridiculous!" Mom said. "For one
thing, three cans of Marvelous Morsels cost more
than a steak!"

"Our puppies have never eaten that fancy

stuff," Lizzie agreed. "I don't even think it's good for them."

"Still," Charles said, "Angela left us a few cans, so we might as well use them up." He didn't know what the big deal was. Sure, it would be easier if Princess just ate Baxter's Beefy Chunks, which Buddy seemed to like just fine. But they had promised to take care of Princess the way Angela wanted them to. Or, at least, *Charles* had promised. He wasn't sure Angela would have left Princess with them if he hadn't. And he really, really wanted to foster Princess.

The tiny puppy was sitting on his lap right now, while the Petersons gathered in the living room. Aunt Amanda had gone home, and the rest of them were looking over Angela's List. "You'll get your Marvelous Morsels," Charles told Princess. He stroked her silky ears. "Don't worry."

Princess did not seem the least bit worried. She just sat there, accepting Charles's pats. Whenever he stopped for even a second, she looked up at him with expectant eyes, lifting one tiny paw and tapping Charles's arm, until Charles started patting her again. Once, when he was saying something to his mom and didn't pay attention to her paw, she gave three short, sharp barks.

Hey, you! More patting, less chatting! Did you forget about me, here on your lap?

"Oops! Sorry!" said Charles as he resumed his patting. Angela had probably patted Princess every time she barked, and now the puppy expected that. It was just like Aunt Amanda had said: It wasn't *Princess's* fault that she was spoiled. Maybe, since she was so young, she could learn to be *un*spoiled — not that Charles knew how to teach her.

Charles gazed down at Princess. He still could not get over how little she was! Tiny nose, tiny ears, tiny, tiny paws. How could any dog *be* so small? She was smaller than Huey, his class's guinea pig! And she hardly weighed a *thing*. If he closed his eyes, he would barely know she was in his lap. But Princess had a big, big personality.

"I don't know how she does it," Lizzie said, shaking her head as she looked at Princess. "She's no bigger than a rat, but it's obvious that she thinks she's better than everyone else, like she's doing us a favor by letting us be in the same room with her."

"Rat?" asked the Bean, who was sitting on the floor with Buddy sprawled across his lap. He stared at Princess, too. "Pincess not a rat! Pincess is a *uppy*!"

"Lizzie didn't mean that Princess *is* a rat," Dad told the Bean. "Princess is definitely a puppy." He made a face. "Sort of," he added under his breath. Like Lizzie, Dad was not a big fan of little dogs. He always said they were "kind of *like* dogs," but "not really good for anything."

"Well," said Mom, who had been reading more of Angela's List, "it's dinnertime, for people *and* puppies. I'm going to start our supper, and Charles, if you're going to feed Princess, you'd better get started, too. It's going to take a while to do it the way Angela spells it out on the List."

"What do you mean?" Charles asked.

Mom didn't answer. She just handed Charles the stack of papers. He groaned. There was no way he had time to read through the whole List right now. He'd better stick to the parts about food.

FEEDING: Part Two

A) Use the pink dishes. The ones with flowers on them are for breakfast; the ones with bunnies are for dinner. Dishes must be washed and dried between meals.

B) Put exactly three tablespoons of Marvelous Morsels Beef-Bacon Bonanza (pink can) into the dish. If it has come right out of the fridge, be sure to microwave on medium for seven seconds. Mash the food with the back of a fork until there are no, repeat *no,* lumps. Not even a small one. Princess does not like lumps.

C) Put the food dish down on its matching pink place mat (flowers for breakfast, bunnies for dinner). Make sure that you have put up Princess's favorite picture (the one of the pink teddy bear) near her eating spot, so she can look at it while she eats.

D) Fill the water dish with one-half bottle of Crystal-Fresh spring water. Do not use any other brand or Princess will not drink it.

E) Call Princess to eat. I usually say, "Princess! Dinny-dins!" or "Princess, time for brekky!"

Charles let the List fall to the floor. "Okay," he said to Princess. "I'll mash your food. I'll put up your teddy-bear picture. I'll pour your spring water. But I am *not* going to talk baby talk to you."

Princess just gazed back up at him with her tiny black eyes, like two shiny buttons. She tilted her head and gave him a puzzled look.

Blah, blah, blah. I don't understand what you're saying — but I do know that I'm still waiting for my dinner. What's taking so long?

Suddenly, Charles had a feeling that he just *might* be talking baby talk, before too long.

Charles was very careful with Princess's dinner. It took ten times longer than pouring out a bowlful of Baxter's Beefy Chunks for Buddy, which he also did. And he was a little nervous about whether or not he was doing everything correctly. But when he called, "Princess, dinnertime!" she came scampering right in, her tiny twinkle-toes just a blur of motion. Princess went right to her pink bowl, on the pink place mat, with the pink teddy-bear picture taped up on the cupboard door above it, and began to eat. She did not seem to notice that he had skipped the baby talk. Maybe Princess wasn't *quite* so fussy after all.

Mmmm, delicious. Not a single lump. Just how I like it.

Charles watched, fascinated, as Princess nibbled daintily at her food and lapped up droplets of water with her tiny pink tongue. It was kind of true what Dad and Lizzie said: A dog this tiny was *like* a dog, but so, so different from what Charles was used to. Compared to Princess, Buddy looked like a jolly giant, chomping away at his Beefy Chunks and then slurping splashily at his dented metal water bowl while his collar tags clanked against the side.

After the puppies had eaten, the Peterson family had their own dinner. Afterward, Charles played with Buddy and Princess in the living room, tossing a ratty old sock monkey for Buddy (it was his favorite toy these days) and a miniature pink tennis ball for Princess. (PLAYTIME: Part One. Princess will play with: A) Her pink tennis ball, or B) The pink butterfly tug toy.) Both puppies had a great time tearing after their toys and prancing back to Charles with their tails held pridefully high and their prizes clutched in their jaws.

Mom came down after putting the Bean to bed and told Charles it was almost his bedtime, too. "And you'd better read this section," she said to Charles, pointing to a spot on the List. He looked down at the page and sighed.

BEDTIME: Part One
A) Princess sleeps in her palace, with her three favorite bedtime toys: her stuffed ladybug, her pink squirrel, and her squeaky saucer....

CHAPTER FIVE

The next morning, Charles decided to try an experiment. Maybe Princess wasn't *really* all that spoiled. After all, he hadn't baby-talked when he'd called her to dinner and she'd still come right away. For breakfast, instead of following the List, he just gave Princess a small serving of Baxter's Beefy Chunks in a regular cereal bowl.

Princess ran right over when he called her. But she took one sniff at the bowl and backed away. She sat down on her tiny behind and barked.

You've got to be kidding me! What is *that stuff?*

Charles got the message. He scraped the food into Buddy's dish (Buddy had already gobbled down his portion) and started over. He found the leftover Marvelous Morsels in the fridge and plopped a couple of spoonfuls into the cereal bowl. "Okay?" he said, putting it down for Princess.

The tiny puppy tippy-toed over to take another sniff. She backed off again and barked some more.

I don't think *so. It's cold, it's lumpy, and it's in the wrong dish.*

Charles picked up the bowl, scraped the food into Princess's pink flowered bowl, stuck it into the microwave for seven seconds on medium, took it out, mashed the food carefully with a fork, and put it down on the pink flowered place mat.

This time, Princess ate every last bite.

By the time Aunt Amanda came to pick him up for their Reading With Rover session, Charles had to admit he was feeling just a little bit overwhelmed by all the work needed to take care of Princess.

"Take *care* of?" Aunt Amanda asked as they drove to the library in her van. Bowser, the golden retriever, was sitting in the way-back. "More like *spoil*. That dog is spoiled, no two ways about it. Angela babied her, and now that's what she's used to. It's going to take a whole lot of work to change Princess into a dog that anyone would want to adopt."

Charles groaned. "I know," he said. "She's so cute and smart and fun. I really like her! But who would want to take her the way she is now?" He groaned again. "I know Mom and the rest of the family won't put up with her for very long. I'm going to have to find her a forever home as soon as I can. And I can't imagine sending Princess to an animal shelter the way she is now, even one as nice as Caring Paws."

"Well, maybe I can help come up with some training ideas," Aunt Amanda said. "I'm sure she can learn to be less spoiled. But right now, we have another job to do." She pulled up in front of the library. "Ready, Bowser?" she said, turning around to look at the big, copper-colored dog.

Bowser gave a happy bark and wagged his tail. Bowser was always glad to do anything Aunt Amanda wanted him to do. He was such a good boy.

Another car drove up as Charles waited for Aunt Amanda to clip on Bowser's leash. It was a red sports car, old and rusty but with a cool convertible top that was down, so Charles could see two people — and a dog — riding in it. "Hey there!" the driver said, popping open the door and hopping out. "You here for the program, too?" He stuck out his hand for a shake. "I'm Harry, and that's Zeke."

He pointed to a huge chocolate-brown Labrador retriever with a red bandanna around his neck. Charles had seen that dog around town before. He also recognized Harry, because Harry played second base for the high-school baseball team. Charles had been to a few of their games with his dad, and everybody in the bleachers had been talking about Harry. Dad said he was a "master of the double play." Harry was a good batter, too. Charles remembered one long, high home run that had practically landed on the school roof!

"Hi," Charles said, feeling kind of grown-up as he shook Harry's hand. "I'm Charles. That's my aunt Amanda, and her dog Bowser. I'm just helping."

"Cool." Harry turned back to the car. "Coming, Nathaniel?" The little boy in the backseat was busy unclipping his seat belt. He didn't look up. "That's my cousin Nathaniel," Harry told Charles. "I tried to get him to read to Zeke, but Nathaniel's kind of quiet, and Zeke is — well, Zeke is energetic. We decided Nathaniel should come along with me and try another dog."

"Bowser might be perfect," Aunt Amanda said. "He's really mellow."

"Excellent!" Harry clipped a black leather leash onto Zeke's collar and opened the car door so the big dog could charge out. Charles stepped back to give him room. Nathaniel climbed out of the car and closed the door carefully, then stood close to Harry, looking down at his own red sneakers. When Zeke tried to give him a big, sloppy kiss, Nathaniel flinched and moved even closer to Harry.

Charles thought of the way the Bean used to try to hide behind Mom's legs when he was feeling shy. He almost expected Nathaniel to stick his thumb into his mouth, like the Bean used to do. But Nathaniel was not a baby. Charles thought he must be at least five: That seemed too old for thumb-sucking.

"Well, let's go meet everybody!" Harry said. He strode toward the library, with Nathaniel trotting to keep up.

Charles watched Zeke amble along next to Harry. Now that was what Lizzie would consider a *real* dog. Harry probably wouldn't think much of a spoiled little brat like Princess. Charles reached out to take Bowser's leash while Aunt Amanda put her car keys in her pocketbook.

It was funny to walk right into the library with a dog. Usually, dogs had to stay outside, tied to a tree or the bike rack while their owners returned books. Even the annual pet show, sponsored by the children's room at the library, took place outside in the courtyard. But today was different. Today, dogs were specially invited.

The children's room was one of Charles's favorite places. First of all, there were all the books you could ever want to read, just sitting there patiently, waiting for you to find them. Second, there were lots of cozy nooks and corners where you could curl up with a book if you wanted to start reading right away, before you even took it home. Third, the librarians were really, really nice. Like Nancy, who greeted Charles and Aunt Amanda as they came in. "Welcome!" she said.

"This must be" — she checked her list — "Bowser? Is that right?"

Bowser woofed and wagged his feathery tail. He was always happy to hear his name.

"Great! Right this way!" Nancy led them to an alcove where the other dogs and people were gathering. "I think we're all here, then," she said, "so I'll read off this list of partners and you can all get down to the business of reading!" She checked a sheet of paper in her hand. "Harry and Zeke, you'll read with Simon."

Harry stood up and waved a hand. "That's us," he said. "I'm Harry, and this is Zeke."

"Yeah!" A chubby redheaded boy in overalls jumped up and ran over to fling his arms around Zeke. Zeke's tail thumped the floor as he licked the boy's cheek. In a second, the two were rolling around happily on the carpet.

"Simon!" Nancy said. "I'm glad you like Zeke, but let's save the wrestling match for another time and place. Today is for reading."

Charles and Aunt Amanda smiled at each other. Zeke had found the perfect partner.

"Amanda and Bowser," Nancy went on, "you'll read with Nathaniel."

Nathaniel didn't run over the way Simon had. He stayed where he was, looking down at the floor. But he did manage a tiny smile when Charles brought Bowser over to meet him. Charles was pretty sure that Nathaniel liked dogs. He suspected he was just a little overwhelmed by them, that was all.

That morning, it was Charles who did most of the reading. Since Nathaniel was a little too shy to read out loud to Bowser, Charles sat down next to the big, happy dog and read him story after story. Bowser's head was in Aunt Amanda's lap, and Nathaniel sat nearby, listening. Once in a while, Nathaniel would reach out and give Bowser a little pat.

"I think Bowser liked *Good Night, Gorilla,* the

best," Nathaniel whispered at the end of the session.

"Maybe next time *you* can read to Bowser," Aunt Amanda said.

"Maybe." Nathaniel did not sound very sure about that. But Charles was sure of one thing: Being a part of Reading With Rover was going to be lots of fun.

CHAPTER SIX

"One lady brought a corgi, and there was a big, huge dog — maybe some kind of St. Bernard mix, and oh, the *cutest* dog was this miniature poodle. Pearl, her name was. She can do all kinds of tricks. I bet she could be in a circus or something."

"What color was the big dog?" Lizzie asked as she passed a heaping platter of spaghetti and meatballs to her dad.

It was dinnertime, and Charles was telling the rest of the family about his excellent day with Aunt Amanda at the Reading With Rover program. Buddy and Princess had already had their dinners, and now they were napping — Buddy under the table and Princess in her pink palace, over in the corner.

Charles shook his head. Lizzie had asked about the other dogs at the program. Trust her to zoom in on the one big dog he had mentioned. "It was mostly white, with some brown patches. The miniature poodle was black. You should have *seen* Pearl when she jumped —"

But Lizzie just wasn't very interested in hearing about a little dog. "How about Bowser?" she interrupted. "Did he have a good time?"

"Definitely." Charles picked one cherry tomato and three chunks of cucumber out of the salad bowl. If he was lucky, that would count as his vegetable.

"Add a piece of green pepper and you've got a deal," his dad said, as if he were reading Charles's mind.

That sounded fair. Charles picked out the smallest piece of green pepper he could find. "Bowser *loved* being around all the people. And everybody loved him, too. Except Nathaniel, maybe. I think Nathaniel was a tiny bit afraid of Bowser."

"Afraid of Bowser?" Lizzie couldn't believe it. "Sweet old *Bowser*?"

"Not everybody loves all dogs the way you do, Lizzie," her mom reminded her. "Some people think dogs, especially big dogs, are a little scary."

"Boooo!" said the Bean, raising up his hands like he was haunting someone. "Scary!"

"Not scary like a ghost," Charles told his little brother. He understood what his mom was saying. "Scary like — well, just scary. Like they think maybe the dog will knock them over, or bite them, or something. Anyway —" He was about to say that he thought Nathaniel would probably get used to Bowser soon, but he was interrupted by Buddy.

Buddy, who was putting his paw up on Charles's knee.

At dinnertime.

Buddy was begging.

Buddy *never* did that. When Mom and Dad had

agreed that the family could keep Buddy, there had been a few conditions. One of them was "no begging." Dad said he hated when dogs begged, because it meant he couldn't eat his own dinner in peace. So the family rule was that nobody *ever* fed Buddy — not even one eensy, minuscule molecule of food — from the table. That way, they never rewarded him for begging, so he never really even tried.

Now, for the first time, here was Buddy, begging. He had a paw on Charles's knee. He had an innocent, adorable *I'm so hungry, please feed me* look in his big brown eyes. And he was even drooling a little bit!

Charles looked over at Buddy's dish. How hungry could he be? He hadn't even finished his whole dinner. "What's up, pal? Tired of Beefy Chunks?" He was joking, but Buddy ran over to sniff Princess's empty dish and then ran back to whine, and paw, and give Charles the "feed me" look. Charles realized that what Buddy wanted wasn't just any food. Buddy wanted some of the food *Princess* had been eating. Buddy wanted Marvelous Morsels.

Please, please? It smells so good I can hardly stand it when she's eating next to me! I want some, too! Please? Please?

Uh-oh.

"Am I seeing what I think I'm seeing?" Dad was frowning as he pointed his fork at Buddy. "Is that dog *begging*?"

"I knew it, I just knew it," said Lizzie. "He's learning bad habits from that spoiled brat Princess."

At the sound of her name, Princess woke up and poked her head out of the palace door. She blinked a little, then barked.

What was that about me? Did I hear my name? Of course *you're talking about me, but how about keeping down the noise? Can't a puppy get some* sleep *around here?*

"Just wait," Lizzie warned. "If he spends much more time around her, Buddy will turn into a yappy dog, just like Princess."

Princess barked again at the sound of her name.

"Really, Lizzie," Mom said. "Princess isn't that bad."

"No, she isn't!" Charles said. Why couldn't Lizzie learn to love Princess? "She's cute, and she's really smart, and —"

Just then, Buddy let out three little barks and put his *other* paw up on Charles's knee. Lizzie made a *"See?"* face, and Charles trailed off. What if Princess really *was* teaching Buddy bad habits? He had to find this spoiled — but wonderful — puppy a forever home. And he had to do it soon.

CHAPTER SEVEN

It was Saturday, and Aunt Amanda and Charles were on their way to the library for the second Reading With Rover session. It had been a little over a week since the tiny Yorkie had come to live with Charles and his family, and the truth was that the Petersons had just about had it with Princess.

Dad said Princess was a good teacher — "a little *too* good" — when it came to the way she had taught Buddy to beg for special treats.

Lizzie was sick of Princess always having to be the center of attention.

Mom was tired of moving Princess's palace all over the house, from the living room, where she napped during the day, to Charles's room, where she slept at night, to the porch, where she had to have it as a resting place during outdoor playtime.

The Bean was acting cranky because *he* wasn't getting enough attention.

Buddy was acting naughty for the same reason.

As for Charles? Charles still liked Princess a lot. But he had to admit that he wished he had never seen the List. He could not believe how complicated it could be to take care of one tiny puppy.

It seemed like Charles had been spending almost all his free time making sure that Princess was happy. Now, even on Saturday, when he had thought he might be enjoying a little break from taking care of Princess, he was not. True, he was with Aunt Amanda. True, they were on their way to the library. But this time, Bowser was not the only dog in the back of Aunt Amanda's van. This time, Princess was there, too, tucked inside her pink palace.

Princess wasn't coming to be part of Reading

With Rover. For one thing, she hadn't been to the training program. For another, it would be too distracting for the kids to have an extra dog on hand. No, Princess was just along for the ride.

It was cool enough outside so she would be safe waiting in the van, as long as it was parked in the shade with the windows cracked open, while Charles and Amanda were in the library. (Charles knew you should *never* leave a dog in a car with the windows up. The inside of a closed-up car can get way too hot for a dog, even if it's not hot outside.)

And, after Reading With Rover was over, Charles and Aunt Amanda were going to take Princess over to Bowser's Backyard for some playtime with other dogs. All of this would give the rest of the Petersons, including Buddy, a much-needed break.

Charles got a break, too. While he was at Reading With Rover, he would not have to think about how to take care of Princess. He would not have to pay attention to picking out a bow that perfectly matched that day's T-shirt (FASHION: Part One) or figuring out which leash went with which collar (FASHION: Part Two). All he had to do was help Aunt Amanda.

When they got to the library, Nathaniel was already there, waiting. He looked happy to see them, even if he didn't run over to throw his arms around Bowser. And once again, Charles ended up doing most of the reading. Nathaniel still seemed to be nervous about sitting too close to the big dog, so he sat on Aunt Amanda's lap while Charles sat next to Bowser, stroking the dog's long, silky ears while he read. Charles noticed Nathaniel watching, and he could tell that Nathaniel really wanted to be petting a dog, too — the little boy just wasn't sure about Bowser yet.

All the other kids seemed to be really into reading to their dogs. Simon lay sprawled on the floor with one arm over Zeke, who was curled up next to him. A girl with braids sat against a bookcase with the corgi's head in her lap. Pearl, the lively miniature poodle, loved being read to so much that she actually sat still, her bright eyes focused on the face of the boy who was reading to her. And the huge St. Bernard mix was being read to by a pair of twins, two boys who had run right over the moment they were assigned to read with him. They lay on top of the enormous dog as if he were a big, furry rug, showing him the pictures as they took turns reading each page.

Charles loved reading to Bowser. He was used to reading to dogs because he read the funnies to Buddy every single Sunday. Lately, Buddy's favorite comic was *Blondie*. Charles did silly voices for all the characters, plus he would describe what Dagwood was wearing, like pajamas with pictures of doughnuts on them, or what Dagwood was eating, like ten-story sandwiches that were *way* too big for anybody's mouth. Buddy always wagged his tail when he heard about the sandwiches, as if he especially loved that part.

That morning at the library, Charles was so happy reading to Bowser that he lost track of time. He was surprised when Nancy announced that it was time to finish up for the day. Nathaniel helped him stack up their books. They brought them to the librarian's desk, and then they walked out, along with Harry, Zeke, Aunt Amanda, and Bowser.

When they got to the van, Aunt Amanda asked Charles to take Princess out for a minute, since the puppy had been waiting so long. "She's probably bored and lonely," she said. "I hope she wasn't barking her head off the whole time we were inside."

"You have another dog in there?" Harry asked. He had already put Zeke into the backseat of his own car, and Nathaniel was busy buckling himself in. "Let's see!"

Charles hesitated. He wondered if Harry would laugh at Princess, in her I'M BEAUTIFUL T-shirt. But he couldn't think of a good excuse for hiding her. So when Aunt Amanda opened the back of the van, Charles reached inside Princess's pink palace and clipped her pink, rhinestone-studded leash onto her pink, rhinestone-studded collar. Then he gathered her into his arms — she hardly weighed a thing! — and turned around to show Harry.

"This is Princess," he said. "She's —" He paused, trying to think of the best way to explain how spoiled she was.

But Harry jumped in before Charles could say another word. "She's a Yorkie!" he exclaimed. "Wow! Is she cute!" He held out his arms, and Charles handed Princess over. "Oh, yes you are!" Harry said, nuzzling the puppy's nose. "You're the cutest, aren't you? And you know it, too!"

Princess licked Harry's chin and wagged her tiny tail.

The cutest? That's me! **Finally,** *someone who understands how very, very special I am. You deserve some kisses. Now, just make sure to keep that attention coming!*

Then Harry looked up and saw Charles staring. He grinned and shrugged. "I happen to like little dogs," he said. "Especially Yorkies. My aunt Maggie — that's Nathaniel's mom — loves them, too."

Hearing Nathaniel's name made Charles remember that the little boy was waiting for his cousin. But when he looked, Nathaniel wasn't in Harry's car! Charles turned around, only to find Nathaniel standing, quiet as a mouse, behind him.

The little boy was staring at Princess, and Charles recognized the look in his eyes. Nathaniel had found a dog he could love.

CHAPTER EIGHT

Back at home, after Reading With Rover, Charles was too busy taking care of Princess all afternoon to think about anything else. But that night, lying in his bed with Princess snoring softly in her palace nearby, he remembered the look on Nathaniel's face when the little boy first spotted the Yorkie. Nathaniel's big smile had said it all.

Nathaniel had played with Princess for a while — right there on the library lawn. He had tossed her miniature pink tennis ball, and she had scampered after it, over and over. Nathaniel had laughed and laughed! Charles thought Nathaniel was like a different kid when he was around Princess. He didn't seem shy at all.

And Princess loved Nathaniel, too. She had jumped right into his lap and licked his face, paying special attention to his nose.

Charles almost felt jealous as he watched Nathaniel and Princess play together. They seemed like they had been friends forever.

Now, in bed, Charles thought about it. And, all of a sudden, he had not just one but *two* really big, really great ideas. Charles's first idea was: Maybe Nathaniel wasn't afraid of dogs after all. Maybe it was just *big* dogs he was afraid of, like Zeke and Bowser. Maybe he would be happier reading to Princess.

And the second, really great idea was: Charles had heard Harry say that his aunt Maggie, Nathaniel's mother, loved Yorkies. Maybe, just maybe, Nathaniel and his mom would turn out to be Princess's perfect forever family!

As soon as he got up on Sunday morning, Charles called Aunt Amanda and told her both ideas. "Well," she said, "as for the first part, I'll have to make a call to find out if it would be all right to bring Princess instead of Bowser next week. After all, she hasn't been through the Reading With Rover training program. But since *I* have, and since Princess actually behaves pretty well as long as someone's holding her and giving her attention, they'll probably say it's okay."

"Great," said Charles. "Then, when Nathaniel gets to know Princess a little better, maybe he and his mom will want to adopt her!" He still thought his second idea was the best one of all.

"I can't help with that part," Aunt Amanda said. "But maybe you should call Harry and ask if he thinks that Nathaniel's mother might want to adopt a dog, before you get too carried away."

Aunt Amanda found Harry's phone number on a Reading With Rover contact list, and Charles called him right up. Charles explained about bringing Princess for Nathaniel to read to, and Harry thought it was a great idea. "Excellent! I have a feeling Natty will really love that," he said.

Then Charles took a deep breath and brought up his other great idea. He explained that he and his family were only fostering Princess, and that they were hoping to find her a forever home soon. If it worked out for Nathaniel to read to her, maybe Nathaniel's mom would adopt the puppy! Then Nathaniel would have his very own dog at home, to read to whenever he wanted.

Also, Princess would be out of the Petersons' hair. Which would be a good thing, considering how everybody in the family was very, very tired of Princess's List. (Of course, Charles didn't say any of that last part out loud to Harry.)

"Wait, Princess is up for adoption? Why didn't you tell me earlier, when we were playing with her?" Harry sounded surprised.

"I didn't really think of it until later," Charles confessed. "But even if I had, I wouldn't have said anything in front of Nathaniel. We have a rule in my family about our foster puppies. Mom says it's not fair to ask kids if they'd like to adopt them — because they'll get disappointed later if their parents say no. We always ask the parents first." Charles took a breath. "So anyway, what about your aunt?"

"I don't know," said Harry. "It's a great idea, but to tell you the truth I don't think it's likely to happen." He sighed. "Did I ever tell you what my aunt does for a living? She's a dog groomer! She works with dogs all day long, so she always says she doesn't want one at home, too." He paused. "But let me think about it. I might be able to come up with a way to convince her. I'll call you back later if I do."

Charles hung up, feeling frustrated. He looked down at Princess, who had been napping in his lap while he made the phone calls. "What are we going to do with you?" he asked. Charles knew that Princess couldn't really understand him, but she looked up at him with her black button eyes and he could guess just how she would answer:

Well, that's *a no-brainer! You'll pat me! And feed me delicious things! And, naturally, give me lots and lots of attention.*

For the next few hours, Charles tried to forget about the Princess problem. Hopefully, Harry would come up with an idea. But meanwhile, Charles just wanted to have a little fun with Princess, instead of worrying about finding her a home.

Right after breakfast, Charles lay on the living room floor and read the Sunday funnies to Buddy and Princess. Buddy lay quietly and listened, his eyes on Charles's face. But Princess kept barking and putting her paw on the newspaper.

Not that one! This one!

Charles laughed and patted Princess's little silky head. "Okay, I guess you don't like *Blondie*. How about *Buckles*? He's a funny dog."

Later, Charles and the Bean ran around in the backyard with both puppies, teaching Buddy and Princess how to play tag. Princess was *great* at being "it." She dashed around, chasing the others into every corner of the backyard.

Finally, when both puppies were tuckered out, Charles sat down to let them both take a nap on his lap. The Bean leaned against Charles, too, drowsily patting first Princess, then Buddy.

A little while later, Mom called from inside, "Charles, you have a phone call!"

Charles nudged the Bean awake but the puppies stayed sound asleep. He carried sleepy Princess and sleepy Buddy into the kitchen with him. Princess was light as a feather, but Buddy was almost getting too big to carry easily. Charles handed both puppies to his mother and picked up the phone. "Hello?"

"Charles, it's Harry," said the voice on the other end. "I think I have a plan!"

CHAPTER NINE

Harry's plan was this: He thought that if his aunt could just see how much Nathaniel and Princess already loved each other, she would be happy to adopt the puppy. Or, as Harry put it, "It would be a done deal!" All they had to do, said Harry, was get his aunt to show up at the library for that week's Reading With Rover session. There, she would see Princess and Nathaniel in action. The rest would "totally be history!"

Charles thought the plan sounded good. He always loved having a plan. Especially a plan that involved some secrecy and plotting, like this one would. "But how will we get your aunt to come to the library?" Charles asked. "I thought she was busy on Saturdays."

"I've got an idea for that, too," Harry said. "Did you know that the Reading With Rover program is having a special day this Saturday? They want parents to come and see their child reading to a dog. They'll watch from that balcony above the children's room, so they don't disrupt the program. You know the place I mean?"

"Sure." Charles had leaned over that balcony many times, looking down on the people below. It was always fun to watch people when they didn't know they were being watched.

"So I'll make sure Aunt Maggie comes. Then, afterwards, she can come down and say hello to Nathaniel and Princess," Harry said. "What do you think?"

"Sounds great," said Charles. "There's just one thing I should tell you —" He was about to explain to Harry about the List, and about how spoiled Princess was. What if Harry's aunt Maggie *did* think Princess was wonderful, and *did* want to adopt her? He had to be honest about the List.

But before Charles could bring up the subject, Harry interrupted. "Okay, then. I gotta run!" he said. "See you Saturday!"

Saturday took a long, long time to arrive. In fact, Charles could not remember a week that seemed to last as long as that one.

Taking care of Princess was a full-time job, and Charles had to do most of the work, except for when he was at school. Mom and Dad agreed to help out during those hours. But Lizzie flat-out refused to follow the List, so Charles was on his own the rest of the time. This foster puppy was Charles's responsibility and Charles's alone.

By the time Saturday rolled around again, Princess was just as demanding as ever. In fact, she refused to eat her breakfast until Charles had mashed her Marvelous Morsels three times — even though he could not see a single lump after the *first* time he'd mashed the stinky stuff. Charles loved Princess, he really did. But he was really hoping that Harry's aunt Maggie would adopt her. And he was really starting to worry that she wouldn't — at least, not once she found out how spoiled Princess was.

But then Saturday finally arrived, and Charles forgot his worries when he and Aunt Amanda arrived at the library. Harry and Nathaniel drove up just as Charles was getting Princess out of the back of the van. Nathaniel unbuckled his seat belt and practically jumped out of Harry's car. "Wow! You brought her!" he yelled, slamming the door behind him. "Yay!" He ran over to Charles. "Harry said you were going to, but I thought he might be teasing."

Nathaniel was smiling and talking fast. This was a different kid from the shy boy Charles had met a couple weeks ago. He wasn't hiding behind Harry's leg *now*! "Nope, not teasing!" he said. "We brought her just for you to read to. How about that?" He took Princess out of her pink palace and gave her a little hug. Then he put her down on the ground and handed her leash to Nathaniel. "Want to walk her inside?"

Princess stood on her hind legs, put her little paws on Nathaniel's leg, and gave a little bark.

Hurray, it's you again! The one who knows how special I am. Excellent! I hope you're ready to give me lots of attention!

Nathaniel picked Princess up and gave her a hug and a kiss. Then he carefully put her down, wrapped her leash around his fist, and started walking toward the library. Harry, Zeke, Aunt Amanda, and Charles followed him. "All right!" Harry said to Charles, slapping him five as they walked. "Princess is here. Step one is completed!"

"What about step two? Is your aunt coming?" Charles asked.

Harry nodded. "She'll be here!"

"There's just one thing I didn't tell you yet," Charles began.

But they had arrived at the library door. Harry ran ahead to pull it open for Nathaniel and Princess before Charles got to mention the List.

Inside, Nathaniel headed straight for a quiet corner, away from all the other readers and their dogs. He settled right in with Princess on his lap, and Aunt Amanda handed him a book. *"Three Stories to Read to Your Dog,"* Nathaniel said, reading the title slowly. "Perfect!" He opened the book.

Fifteen minutes later, Harry caught Charles's eye from across the room and pointed to the balcony. "She's here!" he mouthed.

Charles looked up to see a pretty black-haired woman who looked a lot like Nathaniel. She was leaning on the railing near some other parents, watching Nathaniel read to Princess. And she was smiling.

When it was time for the day's session to end, Nathaniel didn't want to quit. But Harry went over and whispered something in Nathaniel's ear. Nathaniel looked up toward the balcony. "Mom! Mom!" he yelled. "Did you see? Did you see me reading to Princess?"

That night at home, Charles had just finished feeding Princess her dinner when the phone rang. It was Nathaniel's mother, calling to say how much she'd enjoyed watching Nathaniel read to Princess. "Seeing that dog and Nathaniel together was amazing!" she said to Charles. "Where did my shy little boy go? She's *great* for him."

"So —" Charles was almost afraid to ask. "Did Harry tell you Princess is available for adoption?"

"He did — and I'm definitely thinking about making Princess a part of our family," said Maggie. "I know Nathaniel would love that, but I need a little more time to decide if I really have the energy to take care of my own dog after dealing with everybody else's spoiled darlings all day at my grooming shop."

Charles winced. Maybe this was not the best moment to bring up the List. But Maggie kept talking.

"Anyway, I have some thinking to do. But if you bring her to the shop tomorrow, I'll make a decision by then."

She was talking so fast and so excitedly that Charles could not get one single word in. Otherwise, he *definitely* would have gotten around to telling her about the List. At least, he *probably* would have. Wouldn't he?

CHAPTER TEN

A bell jingled as Charles and Harry walked through the door and into the front room of Maggie's Wash and Wag the next morning. Harry's aunt's grooming shop was directly behind her house, connected by a walkway. When Harry and Charles arrived, a lot of dogs started barking — all different barks, from high, quick barks to deep, low woofs.

Charles looked around and took a deep breath of sweet, warm air. "It smells great in here!" he said. "Just like Hair To —" He stopped himself. Maybe he didn't want Harry to know that he got his hair cut at a beauty salon.

"Just like Hair Today, right?" Harry grinned. "That's exactly what I always think!"

"You mean, you get your hair cut there?" Charles asked.

Harry nodded. "By Danielle. She's the best! I've been going to her for years."

"Me, too!" Charles said. He couldn't believe it.

"Wasn't it a bummer when she moved out of Littleton?" Harry asked. "But it's worth driving all the way to Springfield for her. Hey! Maybe next time we should make our appointments at the same time, and you can drive over with me!"

Charles laughed. "That would be awesome!" Charles loved riding in Harry's red convertible. That morning's ten-minute drive from his house to Maggie's grooming shop had not been nearly long enough.

Charles hitched Princess's pink palace higher up in his arms. "So, this is your aunt's shop," he said, looking around. They were in the waiting room, which was decorated with pictures of dogs of every breed. Lizzie would have loved it. "It's a cool place."

"It sure is," Harry agreed. "I've spent many, many Saturdays and after-school hours here helping my aunt." He opened a door marked EMPLOYEES ONLY and called, "Aunt Maggie! We're here!"

"Come on in!" called Harry's aunt. "I'm in the middle of a poodle!"

Charles giggled. That was a funny picture. But he knew what she meant: that she was in the middle of *grooming* a poodle.

Charles followed Harry into the grooming room. The good smell was even stronger in there, and the air was damp. Charles saw high tables where dogs could stand for their haircuts. He saw rolling carts full of different types of scissors, buzzers, and trimmers. He saw spools of ribbon in every color, for putting the finishing touch on dogs that were ready to go home. And he saw Harry's aunt Maggie, standing at a waist-high tub, working a thick lather of white suds through the brown curls of a very wet dog.

"Almost done!" Maggie said. "One quick rinse" — she aimed a sprayer at the dog's side — "and Hershey here will be ready to go under the dryers." She rinsed all the lather out of the dog's coat. Then she helped him climb out of the tub, toweled him off, led him down a ramp, and — standing back for a moment while the poodle shook off, spraying everything in sight with water — finally helped him into a metal dog crate that had a big blue blower attached to it. She flipped a switch and the blower went on with a whoosh. "See you in a few hours, Hershey!" she said, blowing him a kiss. "Good boy!"

She turned to Charles and Harry, wiping some suds off the end of her nose. "Hey!" she said. "You brought her! Great." She came over and bent down to peer into the palace. "Hello there, little one! You sure are adorable."

Inside the palace, Princess wagged her little tail as fast as it could go. She sniffed the air excitedly.

Yes, you're right — I am adorable! It smells just like home in here. And look at all those ribbons! I like it already.

Maggie straightened up. "I've given it a lot of thought," she said. "And I've talked it over with Nathaniel. We've decided that we would definitely like to make Princess a part of our family."

Charles gulped. He had been dreading this moment for twenty-four hours now, including many hours in the middle of the night when he was too worried to sleep. He really was going to have to tell Harry's aunt Maggie about the List. Actually, he was going to have to *show* it to her. He dug into his pocket for the folded, crumpled stack of paper. "The thing is," he began.

"I am so excited!" Maggie interrupted. "It's been ages since I owned a dog. Did I tell you that I had a Yorkie when I was a little girl? Her name was Bitsy, and she was *so* cute and *so* much fun. Even though I have resisted getting a dog for years, I guess I've always really wanted another Yorkie."

"Was Bitsy sp—" Charles wondered if Bitsy was the kind of dog who had a List.

But Maggie was still talking. "And Nathaniel — well, he's beside himself, of course. He has fallen head over heels for that puppy. Last night he went through his whole bookshelf, picking out books to read to her."

"That's great," said Charles. "But —"

"I was thinking that, for today," Maggie said, turning away to pull a rolling table toward herself, "I'd get Princess used to the shop a little, since she'll be spending her days here with me. And since Yorkies need to be groomed regularly, I thought I'd get her used to *that* idea, too. She's too young for a real grooming, but I'll stand her up on the table and give her a tiny trim. Dogs do much better at the groomers if they're used to the routine." She patted the table. "So, let's get her out of her carrier!"

But Charles put the pink palace down. "Wait! I have to tell you something!" he burst out in a rush, before Maggie could say another word.

Harry and Maggie froze. They stared at Charles.

"Oh," said Maggie. "Okay." She raised her eyebrows. "What is it?"

Charles gulped again. He held up a crumpled wad of paper: Princess's List. "See this?" he said. "It's the List, like, with a capital L." He closed his eyes and opened them again. "A list of all the special ways you have to take care of Princess."

Maggie laughed. "It wouldn't be the first List I've seen," she said. "Lots of people give me Lists when they drop off their dogs. What Popsy *must* have for lunch, or why Topsy *must* have a certain kind of music playing in the shop."

"But Princess's List is really long," said Charles. "The thing is, she's really, really spoiled." There. He'd said it. Now Maggie would say she didn't have time for a spoiled dog, and that would be that.

Maggie's face got serious for a moment. "I don't have time for a spoiled dog," Maggie said. Then she saw Charles's worried expression, and she laughed. "Oh, don't worry, I'll still take her. I know *exactly* how to get spoiled dogs *un*spoiled. I've had plenty of practice at it in this job. It just takes a little time and training. And I'm happy to do it, for Nathaniel, and for Princess — and for me."

"Nathaniel!" she called through the door that led to the house. "Princess is here!" She reached down to open the door to Princess's pink palace. "Come on out, little girl!" she said. "You're home!"

Nathaniel came running in just as Princess bounced out of her palace. The tiny puppy ran right into the little boy's arms, and Maggie smiled down at both of them. Charles smiled, too. The tiny Yorkie had definitely found her perfect forever family.

PUPPY TIPS

All dogs deserve to be treated with love and caring. Are you spoiling your dog if you give him special treats, or let her sleep on the bed with you? Not necessarily. The important thing is that your dog has good manners and is a well-behaved member of the family.

But sometimes spoiled dogs — like Princess — can make life miserable for everyone. They might bark or whine when they don't get their way, destroy things that are important to you, or run off when you are trying to call them.

If your dog acts spoiled, you might need some help from a good animal trainer. She won't train your dog — she'll train *you*! With help, you can learn how to help your dog be the best, happiest dog he or she can be.

Dear Reader,

Have you ever known a dog that was spoiled? I have friends who treat their dogs really, really well. Some people cook for their dogs — every day! Other people send their dogs to camp, give them fancy birthday parties, get them massages, or constantly buy them treats and toys. I don't believe any of these dogs are really spoiled — but they sure are happy.

Everybody loves their dogs! What's the funniest thing you ever heard of someone doing for their dog?

Yours from the Puppy Place,
Ellen Miles

ABOUT THE AUTHOR

Ellen Miles is crazy about dogs, and loves to write about their different personalities. She is the author of more than 28 books, including The Puppy Place and Taylor-Made Tales series as well as *The Pied Piper* and other Scholastic Classics. Ellen loves to be outdoors every day, walking, biking, skiing, or swimming, depending on the season. She also loves to read, cook, explore her beautiful state, and hang out with friends and family. She lives in Vermont.

If you love animals, be sure to read all the adorable stories in The Puppy Place series!

Have you read <u>all</u> the Puppy Place books?
Make sure you find out how it began!
Check out:

GOLDIE

Charles woke up with a bad feeling in his stomach. Why? For a minute, he couldn't figure it out. Then he rolled over and looked at his clock. It was 3:46 A.M., and Charles could hear the loud "deedle-deedle-dee" of his dad's pager going off. Mr. Peterson was a volunteer fireman. When his pager went off, there was a fire somewhere in town.

Charles listened to his dad's footsteps going downstairs. Then he heard the slam of a truck door and an engine starting up. He lay there for a while, worrying a little. He decided to stay awake until his dad came home.

But he must have fallen asleep, because when he woke up again, the sun was shining and his clock said it was 7:16. Charles rubbed his eyes and climbed out of bed. Then he raced down to the kitchen and looked out the window.

Dad's red pickup was not in the driveway.

Mom was making French toast while the Bean — Charles's little brother — crawled around on the floor by her feet. The smell of cinnamon made Charles's mouth water. "Is Dad —" Charles began.

"Dad's fine," Mom said. "He called a little while ago. There was a big fire, but everyone is okay."

Charles let out a big breath. It was cool to have a fireman dad, but scary sometimes, too.

"He'll be home soon," Mom told Charles.

"Where was the fire?" asked Lizzie, scuffing her slippers as she shuffled into the kitchen. She rubbed her eyes and yawned. Lizzie was Charles's older sister. It always took her a long time to wake up.

"Out at a farm in Middletown," Mom said.

At this, Lizzie's eyes popped open. "Were any animals hurt?" she asked.

Mom shook her head. "I don't think so." She flipped a slice of French toast. "Set the table, okay?" Mom asked.

That *proved* that everything was okay. What could be more normal than doing chores?

Since there was no reason to worry, Charles decided to ask his favorite question, the one he asked every single morning.

"So *why* can't we have a dog?" he asked.

His mother sighed. "Again?" She pulled the orange juice out of the fridge and filled four glasses and the Bean's purple sippy cup. "Do we have to talk about this every day?"

"Only until we get a dog," Lizzie said, with a sleepy smile.

"First you said we couldn't have a dog because our apartment was too small," Charles reminded his mom. "Then we moved to this big old house, and now there is plenty of room." He followed Lizzie around the table, putting a fork onto every napkin she laid down. "But instead of adopting a dog, we adopted the Bean. "

Charles looked down at the Bean. Sometimes Charles could hardly remember the Bean's real name. It was Adam. But they had called him the Bean ever since he came to live with them when he was a tiny squirmy baby. "Just a little bean," Mr. Peterson had said, and the name had stuck.

The Bean grinned up at Charles and made a little woofing noise. "Even though he *thinks* he's a dog, he's *not*," Charles pointed out. "He's just a kid who likes to crawl around on the floor, beg for food, and sleep on a fleece dog bed."

"And carry his stuffed toys in his mouth," Lizzie added.

"It's a phase," their mom said, the way she always did. "He'll get over it by the time he's —"

"Seventeen," Charles finished, the way their

dad always did. It was their dad's favorite joke. Their mom didn't think it was so funny.

"Anyway," Charles continued, "back then you said a baby and a dog were too much at once. You said we had to wait until the Bean was older. Well, now he *is*. He's two and a half! He's not a baby anymore."

"No, he's not," agreed his mother, a little sadly. She loved babies. And kittens. Just not puppies. Mr. Peterson always joked about his wife being a cat person, not a dog person. Mrs. Peterson always said she didn't see anything wrong with that. She had grown up with cats and she was used to cats. But the other family members were not interested in cats. The rest of the family loved dogs.

"So, why can't we get a puppy?" Charles and Lizzie asked together.

"Jinx," Charles said to Lizzie. "Owe me a favor. You clear the table after we eat."

Lizzie stuck out her tongue. Charles grinned. He *always* said "jinx" first.

"We *will* have a puppy," their mother said. "Someday. When the time is right, and the puppy is right."

"But when will that be?" Charles asked. "When *I'm* seventeen?" Sometimes he felt as if he'd waited *forever* for a dog. It wasn't fair. Everybody *else* had dogs. And nobody wanted one more than Charles and Lizzie and the Bean. Nobody would take better care of a dog, or teach it as many great tricks, or love it as much as they would.

"We'll know," Mom said. "When the time is right, we'll know." She had that tone in her voice, the tone that meant it was time to change the subject.

But Lizzie didn't seem to notice. "If we had a dog, we'd all feel better," she said. "Did you know that dog owners are happier, healthier, and more relaxed than people who don't have dogs? Plus, having a dog teaches kids responsibility. And a dog can help to protect the house and save people from fires."

Mom held up both hands. "Enough!" she cried. "I've heard all your facts before, Lizzie, and I know they're all true. I also know that puppies are a lot of work and cause a lot of mess and trouble." She turned back to the skillet on the stove.

Charles knew what she was thinking. Dogs shed fur all over the place. They chew things. They knock over garbage cans. They bark. There were lots of reasons for not getting a dog. Mom didn't even have to spell it out anymore.

Charles had only taken one bite of his breakfast when he heard his dad's pickup pull into the driveway. A minute later, Dad trudged into the kitchen. His shoulders were slumped, his face was smudged with soot, and his hair was all flattened from being under his helmet.

"Dad!" cried Lizzie, jumping up to hug him.

"Hey, punkin," he said tiredly.

Charles noticed a big bulge underneath his dad's jacket. "What's that?" he asked, pointing.

Then he noticed that the bulge was moving.

Charles came closer. The bulge was squiggling and squirming all over the place.

Dad smiled and pulled the zipper of his coat down a few inches.

"Meet Goldie," he said. Charles saw two chocolate-brown eyes, a pair of floppy ears, a twitching black nose, and a furry, golden face all streaked with soot.

"A puppy!" Charles yelled.